Where's the Boss?

A dog team alone on Alaska's Iditarod Trail

Lois Harter

Illustrated By David Totten

Publication Consultants

PO Box 221974 Anchorage, Alaska 99522-1974

ISBN 1-888125-63-2

Library of Congress Catalog Card Number: 99-067968

Copyright 1999 by Lois Harter
—First Edition 1999—
—Second Edition 2000—
—Third Edition 2001—

All rights reserved, including the right of
reproduction in any form, or by any mechanical
or electronic means including photocopying
or recording, or by any information storage or
retrieval system, in whole or in part in any
form, and in any case not without the
written permission of the author and publisher.

Manufactured in the United States of America.

Foreword

This story is about some friends of mine, Crystal and Toby, extraordinary team leaders. The idea for the story is based on a real incident involving a member of Lois' own family. This is Lois' first book and it took a lot of growls and ankle nipping to keep her headed in the right direction. I think the final product is a wonderful story full of the love that is shared between mushers and their teams. I know you will enjoy it as much as I do.

Vigorous Tail Wags
Zuma, K-9 Reporter

Zuma's Paw Prints may be read at www.iditarod.com

The greenish glow of the northern lights danced across the Alaska sky, like sheer curtains moving in the breeze at an open window. It was a cold, clear night, perfect for mushing along Alaska's famous Iditarod Trail.

Toby thought about all the time that had gone into training for this particular race as he and his teammates padded along the hard trail, mile after frozen mile. All those trips into the wilderness they had made, the shorter middle-distance races they'd run and finally, last year, the Yukon Quest from Fairbanks, Alaska, to Whitehorse in the Yukon Territory of Canada.

He remembered the first time he had been in harness and how the older dogs had laughed when he got tangled in the tug lines. He smiled to himself remembering how scared he was the first time he was put in the lead position. Wow! He had been so proud when the team had followed him on the trail. It had taken three years to pick just the right team of dogs for

this race. Toby puffed out his chest with pride as he thought of where they were, the Iditarod Trail. He had heard other dogs in other races boast that they had run the Iditarod and had envied them. Finally he was here.

Their boss was professional musher Joe Haddock. Joe was a quiet man in his late thirties who had come to Alaska during the pipeline boom. Like so many others, Joe had stayed to make this huge state his home.

Joe and his teams had been competing in two- to five-hundred-mile middle-distance sled dog races for the past seven years. Last year they had entered the Yukon Quest, his first long-distance race and finished in third place. Ever since Toby and his littermates were born, Joe had dreamed of traveling across the state from Anchorage to Nome on the Iditarod. Now, it had become Toby's dream. He wanted to see the lights of Nome almost as much as Joe.

Joe worked summer jobs to support himself and his dog

team, doing just about every-thing from working on com-mercial fishing boats to la-boring on construction jobs. He had built a three-room cabin with a loft on twenty acres of land just north of Trapper Creek, Alaska. The dogs had a large lot behind the cabin and when-ever Joe wanted, he could just step out on his back porch and talk to them. Joe had also built a large

dog barn for use when the weather was really cold or snowy. If they needed it, the barn would be warm and comfortable. The dogs were Joe's life and he was always thinking of better ways to care for them. He was well respected in the sled dog community for his constant attention to his dogs.

Toby was a large dog for a leader, weighing sixty-seven pounds. He had long legs that made him the ideal lead dog for working in deep snow. He was gray and white, with the typical mask and coloring of an Alaska husky and he had a black stripe down the middle of his tail. His big brown eyes missed very little of what went on around him.

Toby looked over at Crystal. He realized that she was dozing as they trotted along. Years of training enable sled dogs to doze even while moving along a trail. Soon Toby would have to jerk Crystal back to full alertness so that he could rest a little himself. But for now, he'd let her dream.

Somewhere up ahead was a checkpoint where they would

have a warm meal and a bed of straw. Toby drooled just thinking of the warm chunks of beef and the tasty broth that he'd have when they stopped. Joe fed his team good healthy food that was cooked until it was just warm enough to have the right flavor. Just the thought of that meal quickened Toby's pace as he moved the team along to the checkpoint.

This was to be the 24-hour layover required by the Iditarod Race rules. Toby had a feeling that something was wrong with Joe. He and Crystal always watched over Joe carefully. They not only loved the man, but they knew that the team needed Joe for their daily care and feeding. During their last stop, Joe had moved very slowly while feeding them and he had not talked and played with them as he usually did. They had heard him coughing and his voice, when he called to them, was hoarse. He couldn't be getting sick, not now! They'd waited so long and worked so hard to make this trip. Maybe with the rest at the checkpoint, Joe would feel better.

Toby looked back over his shoulder to check on the team, making sure that each dog was in line and that no one was in trouble. As he turned back he saw that Crystal had finished her doze and he nodded to indicate that all was well with the team.

But wait a minute— everything was not all right! Something was missing from the mental picture of the team that flashed through his mind. He looked back again trying to figure out what it was that bothered him. His eyes traveled back over each dog in the team checking for limping or other signs of a problem. No, everyone seemed to be okay. His eyes continued back to the sled. Nothing looked wrong with the sled. Then suddenly Toby realized what was bothering him. "Where's the boss? Where's Joe?" He couldn't see Joe anywhere! He wasn't standing on the runners. He wasn't in the basket of the sled. He wasn't running behind the sled. He just wasn't there! Where could he be? Fear gripped Toby as he turned back to Crystal.

"Crystal, stop the team, help me stop the team!" Toby barked. "The boss is gone! Joe is gone!"

"What ...?" Crystal almost stumbled as she jerked her head around to look back at the sled. Sure enough, Joe was not there.

Crystal and Toby brought the team to a stop. Both leaders looked over their shoulders, past the team, past the sled and as far behind the sled as the darkness would let them see. There was no sign of Joe anywhere.

Beauty, the gray and white female running in first swing, whispered, "What's wrong, Toby?" Beauty was still young and easily spooked, but she was becoming a valuable member of the team. She had developed into a good swing dog, lessening the load of turning the team for the leaders. Someday she would be a leader herself.

"I don't know, Beauty. The boss isn't back there on the sled for some reason and we can't see him anywhere!" Toby tried to control the panic that was rising in him. He could not let the team see him out of control; they relied on him to be their leader.

"Oh no!" Beauty cried with a touch of panic in her voice. She was still a little scared at being so far from the home dog yard. They all knew that she needed the firm, reassuring voice of their musher to keep up her confidence. "What are we going to do? Where could he have gone? He just gave us snacks a couple hours ago."

"Now don't you go getting yourself all upset, Beauty," Crystal chastised. "I'll bet he dozed off and fell off the sled. He's probably back there on the trail yelling at himself for not paying better attention. Toby and I have been alone on a trail before and we know just what we need to do." Crystal tried to sound sure of herself. She knew that if Beauty got the rest of the team upset she and Toby would have a hard time controlling them without Joe's guiding hand. "Now we have to turn the team and go find our musher. We need your help, Beauty. We can't swing the team completely around on this narrow trail by ourselves."

The confidence in Crystal's voice calmed Beauty. She settled down and followed the two leaders into their turn. They would find Joe and everything would be all right. She just knew it!

Toby and Crystal guided the team in a full turn to the right, going back down beside the fourteen other dogs and cutting a path past the sled. Each pair of dogs made the turn as the duo in front of them passed alongside. When it came time to swing the sled around, there was barely enough room on the trail, but the dogs pulled together slowly and eased the sled around without spilling it.

Looking down the trail, the leaders still could not see any sign of Joe. Now they'd have to get down to the business of finding the boss. "Not too fast now," Toby called back. "We don't want to run him down when we come up on him. I'll set the pace and everyone keep a lookout to the side of the trail in case Crystal and I miss something."

The team began backtracking on their trail; everyone's eyes searching the trail ahead and on both sides, looking for the boss. Toby would stop the team every now and then and sniff the air, trying to pick up the scent of their musher. Finally, Crystal spotted a dark shape on the trail. "Toby, look up ahead, there is something in the trail," she growled softly to Toby.

Toby slowed the team cautiously. He knew the dangers of the wilderness and did not want to startle a moose or a wolf napping in the trail. Without their master to protect them the team was defenseless against the creatures that roamed the Alaska wilderness. Toby's eyes peered quickly into the darkness that enveloped the trail. Sniffing the crisp night air for anything unusual. Crystal's soft growl brought Toby's attention back to the dark shape lying just ahead of them, "Yes, that's him," she said.

"I see him, but why is he lying in the snow?" Toby replied as he quickened his steps. They stopped beside the hump in the trail that was their musher and beloved friend. Fear gripped the team as the two leaders sniffed at the cold body before them.

"Is he all right?" called Socks. "He isn't moving. He HAS to be all right, he just has to." Panic was rising in his growl.

Toby put his nose close to the musher's face. He dared not breathe until he felt the touch of the boss's breath on his nose. "He's alive," he shouted to the team.

Crystal and Toby quickly licked the snow off Joe's face and nuzzled him, trying to get him to wake up. No luck. "Crystal," said Toby after a few minutes, "we're going to need human help with this. You're a lot faster than I am so you have to go for help while I stay here with the Boss and the team."

Crystal knew that Toby was right but she was still connected to the team and sled. What could she do to get loose? Thinking quickly, she turned to Beauty and told her to help chew through the back straps on her harness so she could get loose from the tugline. Now, mushers are very strict about chewing lines and harnesses. The lines all have cable running down the inside so they cannot break or be chewed. When a team is hundreds of miles from home, there is no way to replace a line or a harness, so the suggestion that Crystal was making was very serious indeed.

"Oh, the boss gets so angry at anyone who chews a line or harness, Crystal," Beauty said hesitantly. "I don't want him to be mad at me and make me stay home next time."

"Now Beauty, don't panic," Crystal replied soothingly. "I think in this case the boss would want you to help. Besides, he isn't awake and won't know that I didn't do it all by myself. Now let's get to work. We need help for Joe before he freezes to death." With that, Crystal reached back and began to chew on the back of her harness. Beauty joined in on the other strap.

While Crystal and Beauty tended to chewing Crystal loose, Toby was trying to figure out what to do for Joe. The first thing they had to do was get him warm. "Crystal, you and Beauty move forward so the other dogs can move up here," Toby said. Sled dogs have two layers of fur that keep them warm in almost any kind of weather. This same fur can help keep a musher warm too. Soon Joe was covered with the furry bodies of his dogs, each one taking care of a part of Joe's body, snuggling as close as he or she could without smothering Joe.

When Crystal was finally free of the line, Toby gave her some last-minute bits of advice. "Whatever you do, don't let any human or dog catch you. Stay just out of their reach, but if they stop chasing you, stop and bark like crazy until they start to follow again. Lead them back here as quickly as you can. We'll take care of the boss as best we can until you get back."

Crystal took one last look at her musher friend and set off down the trail toward the checkpoint they had left earlier that evening. They had traveled about five hours since then, but she could run much faster free of the harness, so she hoped to cut the time down a lot.

Toby felt a twinge of guilt as he watched Crystal disappear into the darkness. He was frightened for her. She was smaller than he was and would not be able to defend herself if she encountered the wolf pack Toby had caught scent of earlier that night. But what could he do? He was the only one who could handle the team and Crystal was faster than any of them.

For the team waiting with Joe, the hard part had begun. There was nothing left for Toby and his teammates to do but try to insulate their boss from the severe arctic night. Toby curled himself up near the face of his lifelong friend, checking every now and then to make sure he was still breathing. He dozed a little but still heard the whispers of the team members as they waited for help to come.

Socks was talking quietly to his teammate, Sweetpea. "I don't know what I'd do if something happened to the boss. I can't imagine giving up running the trails, but my heart wouldn't be in it with any other musher."

"He's going to be all right, Socks," replied Sweetpea fiercely. "I know it looks bad, but we can't give up. We can take care of him until Crystal brings help."

Yuma, who ran in wheel position, raised his head and listened intently to the night sounds. Somewhere in the distance, he could hear the howl of a wolf. Soon he heard another wolf begin his song and before long, a chorus of wolves was singing its lonely song.

The hairs on Digger's back stood almost straight up as he listened. "I hope the wolves are not on a hunt tonight with Crystal out there all alone." Toby tensed as he heard Digger echo his thoughts; "Pipe down!" he barked. He knew he had to keep the team calm.

Crystal flew along the hard, fast trail toward the last checkpoint. It seemed like she had been running for a very long time and she had no idea how much longer it would take to reach help. She could hear the howling of a pack of wolves and knew that she would be easy game should they decided to attack her. She wanted to increase her speed but knew that to do so might tire her too soon. Her thoughts turned back to her musher and she promised him silently that she would bring a human to take him to safety.

Suddenly, up ahead, she saw a light bobbing in the distance. She knew it was too soon to be a checkpoint. Besides, there were lots more lights at a village. "Could it be a musher's headlight?" she thought as she slowed her pace and studied the light more closely.

As she drew closer, she spotted the lead dogs of another team. Thank goodness! Her heart raced with joy. Now she could talk to a veteran of the trail. She slowed her pace even more, carefully moving forward so as not to appear as a threat to the approaching team.

Finally, she stopped in the trail and shouted to the other team, "My musher is in trouble up ahead and we need help. Can you bring your musher?"

Foxy, a veteran leader of five previous Iditarod races, knew the code of the trail—compete in the race, but when there's trouble, help. He relayed the information to his teammates as Crystal began to bark her frantic message to the approaching musher. Startled, the musher, Michael O'Donald, put his foot on his brake only to find that his team didn't want to stop. They kept pulling against the brake! "Whoa dogs, whoa now!" he shouted to his team.

Mike was finally able to bring his team to a stop. He set his snow anchor to hold the team in place. It is unusual, but not un-heard of, for a dog to be loose and running on the trail. Some-times, the dog is a village dog that has wandered out into the wilderness and become lost. Other times, it is a dog that has somehow gotten loose from one of the racing teams. Most of the time, another musher will just catch the dog and take it to the next checkpoint.

However, if the dog is from one of the Iditarod teams and its musher arrives at the next checkpoint with-out it, the musher will have to scratch. Ac-cording to the rules, a musher must arrive at the next checkpoint with the same dogs he left the last check-point with. "Well, whatever the reason," thought O'Donald to himself, "this dog needs to be gotten back to civilization. Never let it be said that Michael O'Donald isn't a true Alaskan musher. I'll have to catch the dog and put it in my sled and take it with me."

By now all of Mike's dogs were barking and looking at him. They were jumping and lunging, trying to get the sled moving. "Come on Mike!" they shouted.

Mike didn't seem to understand the urgency. He walked to the front of the team and called softly to the dog on the trail. Crystal stopped, turned and looked back at him. She took a few steps toward the musher. Mike thought she was going to come right to him and started to walk toward her. Crystal backed up, barked twice, turned and ran a few yards down the trail. After Crystal repeated this process several times, Mike thought, "That looks like Crystal, one of Joe Haddock's leaders. He left the last checkpoint two or three hours ahead of me." He called to Crystal in a friendly voice, "Come on Crystal, ole gal, come ride in my sled until we catch up with Joe."

Crystal remembered Toby's warning and was not about to allow herself to be caught. She continued to come close, bark and run a little way up trail until finally Mike realized that there was a pattern to Crystal's behavior. "By golly, I think she's trying to tell us something, fellas. Could be Joe's in trouble up ahead. I'd better follow Crystal and find out what's going on."

Mike ran back and jumped on his sled. He yanked out the snow hook and shouted, "Let's go, team!" He didn't have to repeat himself because his team leaped ahead to follow closely behind Crystal.

Meanwhile, the team was doing their best to take care of Joe. Clyde, another leader, asked Toby to check for breathing again, and the team tensed, waiting for the answer. "He is still breathing," Toby called back. "and he seems a bit warmer than when we first got here, too. I think he will be all right. If Crystal can just bring back a human to help."

It was several hours after Crystal had started out when Toby heard barking in the distance. He jumped up and turned to look down the trail. Sure enough, he could see a headlight in the distance and there was Crystal charging down the trail toward them. At last, help was here.

At three thirty in the morning, a musher pulled into the checkpoint with another musher in his sled. The checkers woke up a veterinarian who was also a paramedic and they got Joe inside a warm building.

Joe's team had followed along behind Mike with Crystal resting in the sled. Now they stopped in front of the checkpoint to wait for a human to show them what to do next. Once Joe was inside, checkpoint personnel took the team to the parking area where beds of straw were made for them and warm bowls of meat and broth were

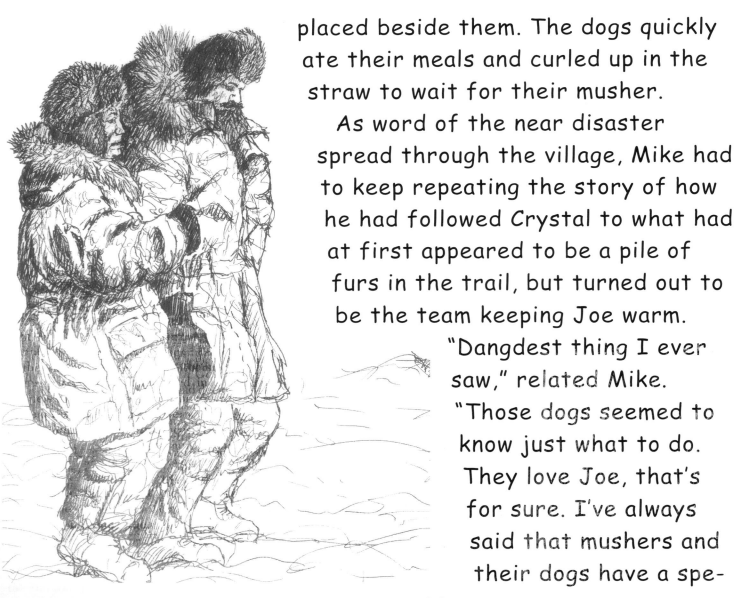

placed beside them. The dogs quickly ate their meals and curled up in the straw to wait for their musher.

As word of the near disaster spread through the village, Mike had to keep repeating the story of how he had followed Crystal to what had at first appeared to be a pile of furs in the trail, but turned out to be the team keeping Joe warm.

"Dangdest thing I ever saw," related Mike. "Those dogs seemed to know just what to do. They love Joe, that's for sure. I've always said that mushers and their dogs have a special bond and those dogs have just proved it. Joe would have died if it hadn't been for his team covering him like that."

Even though everyone knew that what Mike said was true, they still were astonished at the fact that the dogs had known they had to keep Joe warm.

Meanwhile, Joe's team lay in their beds of straw and spoke softly among themselves. "He IS going to be all right." Beauty stated. Crystal smiled to herself as she sensed the new found confidence in Beauty.

"He has to be," answered Crystal. "I wouldn't want another human for my musher."

"We will be sent home," Toby told the team with a little sadness in his voice. There went his dream of seeing the lights of Nome, at least for this race. "I'm sure Joe isn't going to be able to go on, but he WILL be all right."

"I think we should all try to get a little rest," suggested Crystal, knowing that none of them would really be able to rest until they knew what had happened to Joe.

Several hours later, Toby heard footsteps in the snow. He called softly to the team, all of whom were only dozing fitfully waiting for some sign of their musher. One by one the dogs stirred, stood, and looked up to see Joe, bundled in heavy outdoor gear, and aided by a race veterinarian, making his way slowly toward his team. The team went wild, barking and jumping, straining to reach the hand of the man they called friend and "boss."

They wouldn't be finishing this race. Joe had pneumonia and could have died in the cold. He would have, too, if the dogs hadn't known just what to do. As Joe knelt slowly to pet and mumble words of love and thanks to his loyal friends, Toby glanced longingly up the trail towards Nome. Even in his happiness that his musher would be all right, Toby felt a sadness at not finishing the race. However, he knew that there would be many more adventures with Crystal, Beauty, Yuma, Digger, the team, and their beloved friend Joe …. but those are stories for another time.